I0843156

HARPER
GETS GROOMED AT HOME

For Harper, my dog,
who taught me unconditional love and
responsibility from a young age.
You are the reason I started my dog
grooming business.
And for my sons,
Talib and Amir,
the driving force behind my constant pursuit
of growth. Because of you,
I never settle or grow comfortable.
I am always pushing boundaries,
fueled by your existence.

Hi! I'm Señorita Harper, a shy bulldog from Colombia but now living in New York City with my mama. The smells of the city are so different from home big, busy, and a little too noisy for my taste. But when I'm with Mama, I feel safe and cozy.

"Ohhh, Harper, mami!" Mama calls. I wag my stubby tail and spin in circles. The floor feels cool beneath my paws, and I get dizzy with excitement! I look up at her, my ears perked, waiting for her usual words. But instead, she smiles and says, "You're getting groomed today! You're going to smell so good!"

OH NO! I can't! I won't! I feel so ANXIOUS, that's when I feel nervous or unsure of something. My paws scramble against the cool wooden floor as I dart to my soft, warm bed, burying myself under the cozy blankets. The smell of my bed, like fresh laundry mixed with a hint of my favorite treats, comforts me. I wish I never had to go to that loud salon again.

The memory hits me hard: the chaos of the last visit. The sharp scent of wet dogs and shampoo fills the air. The barking so many dogs, each with a voice louder than the last echoes in my ears. The hum of dryers and the sharp spray of water make my heart race.

It was OVERSTIMULATING, this happens when so many things are happening at once and it's hard for your brain to focus and calm down. I want to hide, but most of all, I just want Mama.

I snap back into reality and see Mama walking over. I look up and she gives me a soft, gentle rub on my head. "Harper, don't worry sweetie," she says. "This time, the salon is coming to you!"

Suddenly, I hear a knock on the door, and Mama yells, "One second!" She opens the door, and in walks a girl carrying a huge bag.

My nose twitches she smells nice, like fresh soap and treats! I walk over and sniff her legs.

Mama smiles and says, "This is your new groomer Ashley. She's going to groom you at home today. You're going to smell so fresh and clean when she's done!"

I feel a little INTIMIDATED, this feels like I'm up against something that is much bigger than me and makes me feel afraid. I slowly back away toward my bed. This is so new, and I don't know what to expect.

Ashley walks over and crouches down to my level, her voice soft and calm. "I know this can be a little scary" she says "but I promise it'll be quick and don't worry, Mama is here with you. We've got your favorite treats too! You can even sit on my lap the whole time if you want!"

Her voice feels soothing, like a warm blanket wrapped around me. She reaches out and gently pets my head. I start to feel RELIEVED, which feels like a big sigh of 'phew' all my worrying starts to wither away and I feel okay again.

We head to the bathroom. "You like treats, right? Want some before your bath?" Ashley asks. I scamper over, my paws tapping lightly on the tiled floor, and she gives me five of my favorite treats. Yum! Sweet and crunchy, they're just what I needed to calm my nerves.

She picks me up, the cool tub feeling cold against my paws as she gently places me in. I'm surrounded by the scent of soap clean, fresh, and a little like flowers. It's comforting, she washes me up and rinses me off.

She sits down, and I crawl between her warm legs, the soft fabric of her pants against my fur. She dries me up with a warm fuzzy towel. Then, she pulls out the big hose and the sight of it makes me freeze. It looks so huge and strange, and I feel a little TIMID, this is another word for scared.

"It's okay," she says softly, her hand gentle as it rubs my back. "This is just the dryer it's loud, but it'll feel good!" The air around me feels cool, and I can hear a low hum start to build up. Then the noise blasts into my ears loud and powerful like a storm, but her calming voice and the warmth of her hands help me stay still.

I start to feel safe again as she pets my back and dries me. Mmmm, this feels so warm and nice. "You're all dry!" she says with a smile, handing me more treats.
"Now, let's brush your teeth!" she says, pulling out a toothbrush. It tastes just like chicken, my favorite, yum!

"Last thing your nails!" She shows me the nail clipper. "It'll take just a minute, and then you can go back to Mama!" I get nervous again but this time I SELF REGULATE, this is when I take a few deep breaths and remind myself that I am safe and in control of my feelings. "All done!" Ashley says.

Wow, that was so much better than the salon! I can still smell the fresh soap in my fur and feel the warmth from the dryer on my skin.

I see Ashley packing up, and I don't want her to leave. She was so nice to me. I run over and nuzzle my head against her leg.

"Harper, you were so brave!" she says, her voice full of praise, and leans down to pet me. "I'll see you next month!"

I give a little wiggle of excitement, the air around me feeling lighter and happier now. As I run to Mama, I feel the cool breeze from the open windows and hear the soft swish of the trees outside the smell of fresh air fills my nose, and I can't help but feel the happiness in my tail, wagging so hard I almost lose my balance.

"Harper!" Mama calls, her voice full of love.

"You look and smell so good, I can't wait to snuggle with you in bed!". I give her a big lick, and we both curl up on the bed. I feel CONTENT, that's a peaceful feeling when everything feels just right.
It's the best day ever and I can't wait to get groomed at home again.